The Haunted Forest is scared too!

It's dark, windy

and cold outside.

The forest listens to

the midnight

sounds especially

during the

Halloween month.

The forest is

familiar with the

thing's nature

creates. The wild

animals preying on

anything that

comes their way is

a normal sound to

the forest trees.

With the cold air

that blows through

the forest, the trees

shiver and shake

their branches

letting the leaves

fall off and onto the

ground. But that's

not the only reason

the forest shakes

and shivers.

Different sounds

that screech and

echo through the

forest is not

normal to them but

is expected this

time of year.

Shadows appear all

over and move

slowly throughout

the forest making

those different

sounds as they

walk about.

This one tree called

Sappy, has been

around for 100

spooky years.

Sappy knows

that it's very scary

in the forest when

the unknown

happens. There is

howling's,

whimpers and

chilling roars which

are heard among

the forest and

sometimes seen.

When this

happens, the forest

becomes a different

place with all the

scary things that

come and appear at

Halloween. The

forest stays quiet

so they can listen

but also, the forest

can come alive to

scared to stand

still.

There's a shadow

approaching the

forest and Sappy

alerts the trees that

it's coming and

knows by the shape

of the shadow that

this is not a good

one. The shadow is

very dark with horn

like ears and the

footsteps are heavy

with a slow pace. It

moves quietly

making its way

deeper into the

forest creeping

about here and

there crunching the

leaves under its

feet.

The trees are quiet

for now, while the

shadow steps into

the forest. The

forest waits until

the shadow is deep

in the trees so that

it will give the

shadow a lost

sense of direction

when the trees

make noise to

protect themselves.

There is a scream

that sounds

shrilling too the

forest and the trees

start to shiver and

shake their

branches.

Sappy breaks one

of his limbs so loud

that the shadow

begins moving in

circles trying to

find out who is in

the forest with

them. The shadow

pulls out an object

and starts slashing

it amongst the

forest's existence,

not knowing where

the sound of

Sappy's limb came

from in this dark

forest of tall trees

that is everywhere.

The trees all shake

making it difficult

and confusing for

the shadow to hear

anything but the

breaking sounds of

the tree's limbs.

The forest is scared

as to what will

come next by this

dark horn like

shadow thrashing

that object in the

midnight air.

A loud chilling roar

comes from the

shadow and the

forest becomes

quiet with fear.

Sappy reacts

quickly by reaching

out a branch to

knock the shadow

over. The forest

stays silent

wondering what to

do next.

34

After a few

moments, the

shadow stands up

looking around to

see nothing but

dark space. The

forest starts

shaking again

afraid of this

shadow that lurks

within its space.

From a distance

coming into the

forest, a smaller

shadow appears.

Oh no, this is not

good!

A whining sound

comes from this

shadow that's

stepping closer and

closer. The forest

becomes still

watching and

waiting for the two

shadows to join one

another. The two

meet up and with a

loud howling

whimper that only

the two shadows

understand. The

forest begins to

lightly shiver their

branches escorting

the two shadows

out of the forest as

quickly as possible.

A faint sound

comes from the

edge line of the

forest directing the

shadows out as

well. The forest sits

calm and quiet

waiting on the

next event to come

as it happens every

night in October

when Halloween

becomes alive with

many scares in and

out of a haunted

forest.

47

The forest is scared

but defends itself

when it has too.

Whatever has to be

done to keep

intruders out and

so, the forest waits

until the next time

something comes.

The most frightful

thing that occurs is

when a group of

shadows come into

the forest breaking

the sticks off the

tree's branches. On

Halloween night

this was exactly

what occurred

again.

The shadows came

from each side of

the forest moving

around like they

own it. The wind

helps the trees

make noises to

scare off the

intruders, but it

does not always

work. The shadows

are lurking about

and the sound of

them echoes

through the forest

with the footsteps

of the shadows

traveling through

the crisp fall leaves.

There are five

shadows this time

moving through the

forest talking to

one another softly

as if they have a

plan.

The trees rattle

their almost bare

branches slapping

them against one

another trying to

scare the dark

shadows. The

shadows pay no

mind to the forest

noises and go

about their

business.

A couple of the

trees stand in silent

as the shadow's

climbs up them.

Sappy is one of

those trees that the

shadows are

climbing. He

shivers a bit then

sends a chilling

trimmer down its

bark that lay upon

the limbs which

scares the shadow

off. The whistling of

Sappy's thinner

limbs sends a

shrieking noise

throughout the

forest. The other

trees follow Sappy's

whistle and within

a minute, the

shadows creep out

of the forest

crunching the

leaves under their

feet as they run

away scared.

Sappy was named

by a farmer in 1902

when the famer

found his lost dog

laying against the

trunk of Sappy's

tree. The farmer

named the tree

Sappy because his

dog had spots of

sap on his fur. The

farmer believed

that a tree's sap is

a sign of protecting

something. The

farmer returned the

favor and protected

Sappy by declaring

the forest as a

reserve on his land.

The unknown

forest is scary

around this time of

year to humans

and to the trees

because of different

sounds and events

that usually occur

during October

which nature don't

create. It's dark, it's

spooky and its

shapes are creepy!

The dark endless

forest and its own

natural sounds

among it are

frightening to

anything that

comes into them.

Walking along the

forest paths to get

to another side or

space during the

month of October is

scary with its

movement in the

night sky and its

darkness. Walk in

one on Halloween

night and feel your

body shiver from

fright with the

forests darkness

and mysterious

noises that happen

throughout this

scary night and

remember The

Haunted Forest is

scared too!

From the Author

Thank you to all my readers who love to sit and read a short fun book. I have written many short stories for children and to adults who are traveling or just have a short time to wait for something and who needs a good book to pass the time.

Made in the USA
Columbia, SC
09 October 2022

68819683R00046